1299

J F RIC

SEP 06 2001

Ricci, Christine

Prairie dog rescue

Prairie Dog
Rescue

by Christine Ricci
illustrated by Ron Zalme

Ready-to-Read

Simon Spotlight/Nick Jr.
New York   London   Toronto   Sydney

Based on the TV series *Nick Jr. Go, Diego, Go!*™ as seen on Nick Jr.®

SIMON SPOTLIGHT
An imprint of Simon & Schuster Children's Publishing Division
1230 Avenue of the Americas, New York, New York 10020
Manufactured in the United States of America
First Edition
2 4 6 8 10 9 7 5 3 1
Cataloging-in-Publication Data is available for this title from the Library of Congress.
ISBN-13: 978-1-4169-3363-2
ISBN-10: 1-4169-3363-8

Hi! I am 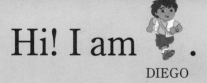.

DIEGO

I am on the prairie

with Mama and

PRAIRIE DOG

Papa .

PRAIRIE DOG

live underground

PRAIRIE DOGS

in a  .

BURROW

They can hide there if

they are in danger.

Oh, no!

I think I hear a !
COYOTE

are afraid of !
PRAIRIE DOGS   COYOTES

Mama  and
PRAIRIE DOG

Papa  need our help.
PRAIRIE DOG

We have to get their five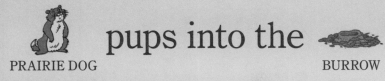
PRAIRIE DOG pups into the BURROW
to keep them safe from
the COYOTE.

There are lots of
animals on the prairie.
I see an and an .

ARMADILLO   OWL

Do you see any pups?

PRAIRIE DOG

Look! Two pups

PRAIRIE DOG

are eating 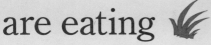 .

GRASS

The is getting closer!
We need to find the other

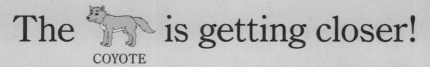 pups.

PRAIRIE DOG

We need to call them.

Say "Yip, yip!"

Two more PRAIRIE DOG pups

heard our call.

They are jumping and

barking.

We need to carry
the pups.
PRAIRIE DOG
My can turn
RESCUE PACK
into anything I need.

Should we use a ,
BOAT

, or a  to carry
SKIS   WAGON

the  pups?
PRAIRIE DOG

Yes! A !
WAGON

How many  pups have we found?

PRAIRIE DOG

One, two, three, four.

We need to find five

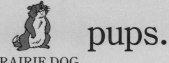 pups.

PRAIRIE DOG

One is still missing.

We need to use

my to look

SPOTTING SCOPE

for the last 🦫 pup.

PRAIRIE DOG

Do you see him?

There he is!

Oh, no!

The  COYOTE is getting closer

to the PRAIRIE DOG pup.

Which path should the

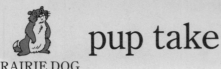

PRAIRIE DOG

pup take

to get to our  ?

WAGON

Hooray!

We found all five pups.

PRAIRIE DOG

PRAIRIE DOGS put a big pile of 🪨 **DIRT** at their 🕳️ **BURROW** so they know where it is.

Do you see the biggest pile of 🪨 **DIRT**?

That is the 🕳️ **BURROW**!

Mama 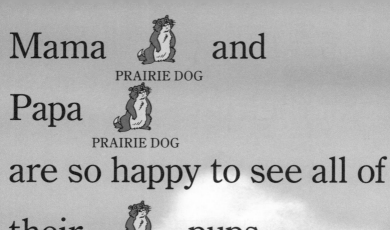 and
Papa
PRAIRIE DOG

are so happy to see all of
their pups.

PRAIRIE DOG
PRAIRIE DOG

Look!

Here comes the  COYOTE !

We have to hurry.

All of the PRAIRIE DOGS

are safe inside the .

BURROW

The is gone.

COYOTE

Rescue complete!